IF
I RAN
the CIRCUS

17 19 20 18 16

ISBN-13: 978-0-00-716990-0

© 1956, 1984 by Dr. Seuss Enterprises, L.P.
All Rights Reserved
First published by Random House Inc.,
New York, USA
First published in the UK 1971
This edition published in the UK 2003 by
HarperCollins*Children's Books*,
a division of HarperCollins*Publishers* Ltd
77-85 Fulham Palace Road
London W6 8JB

Visit our website at:
www.harpercollins.co.uk

Printed and bound in Hong Kong

"**I**n all** the whole town, the most wonderful spot
Is behind Sneelock's Store in the big vacant lot.
It's *just* the right spot for my wonderful plans,"
Said young Morris McGurk, "...if I clean up the cans."

"Now a fellow like me," said young Morris McGurk,
Could get rid of this junk with a half hour's work.
I could yank up those weeds. And chop down the dead tree.
And haul off those old cars. There are just two or three.
And *then* the whole place would be ready, you see..."

All ready to put up the tents for my circus.
I think I will call it the Circus McGurkus.

The Circus McGurkus! The World's Greatest Show
On the face of the earth, or wherever you go!

The Circus McGurkus! The cream of the cream!
The Circus McGurkus! The Circus Supreme!
The Circus McGurkus! Colossal! Stupendous!
Astounding! Fantastic! Terrific! Tremendous!
I'll bring in my acrobats, jugglers and clowns
From a thousand and thirty-three faraway towns
To the place that you'll see 'em in, ladies and gents,
Right behind Sneelock's Store, in the Great McGurk tents!

And I don't suppose old Mr. Sneelock will mind
When he suddenly has a big circus behind . . .

After all, Mr. Sneelock is one of my friends.
He might even help out doing small odds and ends.
Doing little odd jobs, he could be of some aid . . .
Such as selling balloons and the pink lemonade.
I think five hundred gallons will be about right.
And THEN, I'll be ready for Opening Night!

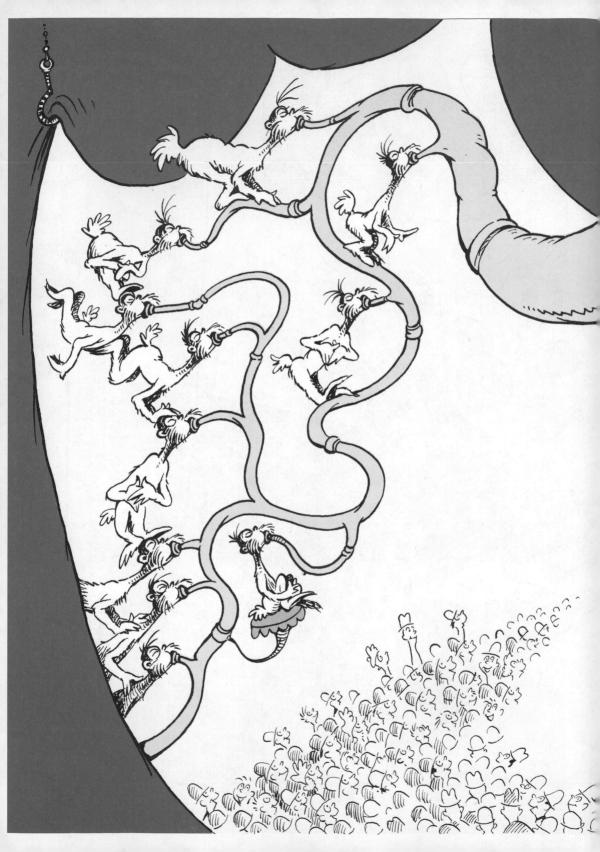

What an Opening Night!
What a night!
What a sight!
I'll hoist up the curtains! The crowds will crowd in!
And my Circus McGurkus will promptly begin
With a welcoming toot on my Welcoming Horn
By my horn-tooting apes from the Jungles of Jorn
Where the very best horn-tooting apes are all born
'Cause the very fresh air there is fine for their lungs.
And some of those fellows have two or three tongues!

This way! Step right in! This way, ladies and gents!
My Side Show starts here in the first of my tents.
When you see what goes on, you'll say no other circus is
Half the great circus the Circus McGurkus is.
Here on Stage One, from the Ocean of Olf
Is a sight most amazing—a walrus named Rolf
Who can stand on *one whisker,* this wonderful Rolf,
On the top of five balls! Two for tennis, three golf.
It's a marvellous trick, if I say so mysolf.

And on Stage Number Two
Here is something quite new!
From a country called Frumm
Comes this Drum-Tummied Snumm
Who can drum any tune
That you might care to hum.
(Doesn't hurt him a bit
Cause his Drum-Tummy's numb.)

And you'll now meet the Foon! The Remarkable Foon
Who eats sizzling hot pebbles that fall off the moon!
And the reason he likes them red hot, it appears,
Is he greatly enjoys blowing smoke from his ears.

Of course pebbles like this are quite hard to collect
But Sneelock will manage, somehow, I expect.
After all, Mr. Sneelock is one of my friends
And I'm sure he'll help out doing small odds and ends.

And on Stage Number Four, see the Wily Walloo
Who can throw his long tail as a sort of lassoo!
With a flip of the hip, with a tail of this kind
He can capture whoever is standing behind!
He can capture old Sneelock. I'm sure he won't mind.

And now here is a Hoodwink
Who winks in his wink-hood.
Without a good wink-hood
A Hoodwink can't wink good.
And, folks, let me tell you
There's only *one* circus
With wink-hooded Hoodwinks!
The Circus McGurkus!

The Show of All Shows!
There's no other Showman
Who shows you a show with a Blindfolded Bowman!
The Blindfolded Bowman from Brigger-ba-Root,
The world's sharpest sharpshooter. *Look* at him shoot!
Through the holes in four doughnuts!
Two hairs on a worm!
And the knees of three birds
Without making them squirm!
And, then, on through a crab apple up on the head
Of Sneelock, who likes to help out, as I've said.

And, now, come to this spot
Where the spotlight is hot
And you'll see in the spotlight
A Juggling Jott
Who can juggle some stuff
You might think he could not . . .
Such as twenty-two question marks,
Which is a lot.
Also forty-four commas
And, *also,* one dot!
That's the kind of a Circus McGurkus I've got!

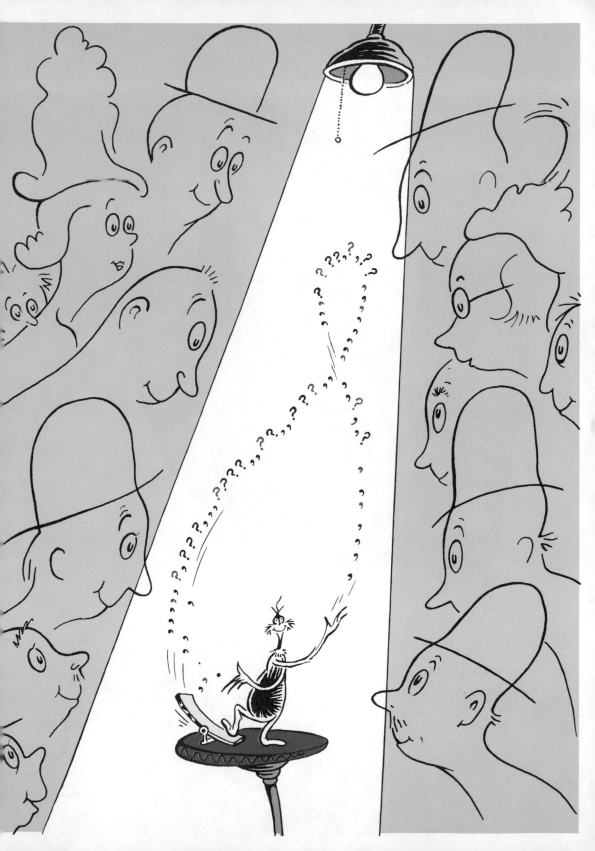

But that's just my Side Show. A start. A beginning.
This way to the Big Tent! You'll find your head spinning.
Why, ladies and gentlemen, youngsters and oldsters,
Your heads will quite likely spin right off your shouldsters!
So hurry! Step lively! Quick, ladies and gents!
And get in to your seats in my Tent-of-all-Tents!
My Parade-of-Parades is about to commence!

You'll see Drum Major Sneelock fling-flang his baton
And my Organ-McOrgan-McGurkus come on
With its hot steaming pipes of gold brass-plated tin
Snorting all sorts of snorts in a bummbeling din
That is super-Stoo-Pendus! Stoo-Mendus! Stoo-Roarus!
And, when I play *Dixie,* please join in the chorus.

Then a fluff-muffled Truffle will ride on a Huffle
And, next in the line, a fine Flummox will shuffle.
The Flummox will carry a Lurch in a pail
And a Fibbel will carry the Flummox's tail
While, on top of the Flummox, three Harp-Twanging Snarp
Will twang mighty twangs on their Three-Snarper-Harp
While a Bolster blows bloops on a three-nozzled bloozer!
A Nolster blows floops on a one-nozzled noozer!
And *then* comes a lion who's partly a trout!
Then *more* stuff! For forty-five minutes, about!

And THEN, behind *them,* then,
While everyone stares
Come my To-an-Fro Marchers
Who march in five layers!
The Fros march on Tos
And the Tos march on Fros.
Don't know how they do it,
But that's how it goes.

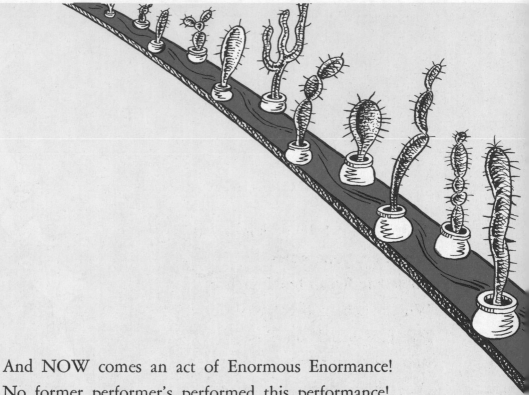

And NOW comes an act of Enormous Enormance!
No former performer's performed this performance!
This stunt is too grippingly, slippingly fright'ning!
DOWN from the top of my tent like greased lightning
Through pots full of lots of big Stickle-Bush Trees
Slides a man! What a man! On his Roller-Skate-Skis!
And he'll steer without fear and you'll know at a glance
That it's Sneelock! The Man who takes chance after chance!
And he won't even rip a small hole in his pants.

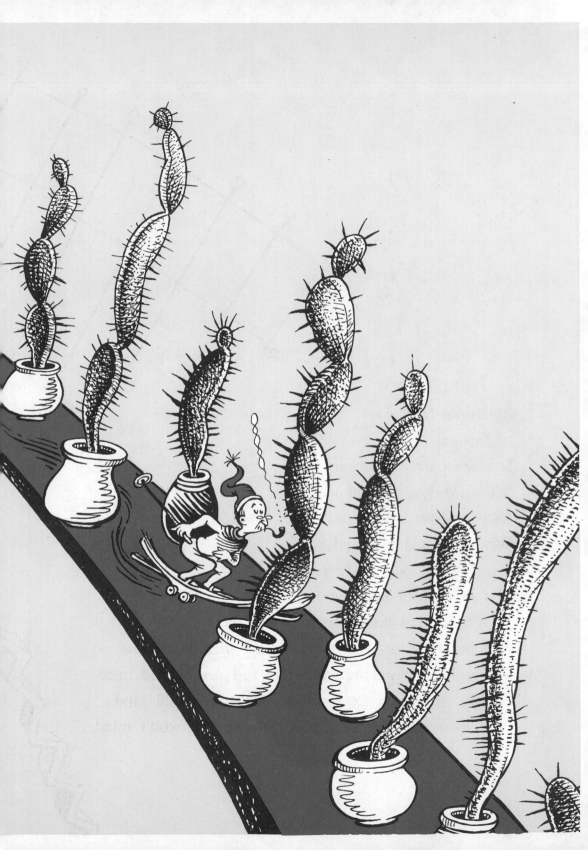

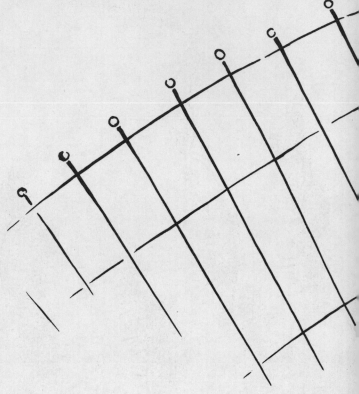

And now *Here!*
In this cage
Is a beast most ferocious
Who's known far and wide
As the Spotted Atrocious
Who growls, howls and yowls
The most bloodcurdling sounds
And each tooth in his mouth
Weighs at least sixty pounds
And he chews up and eats with the greatest of ease
Things like carpets and sidewalks and people and trees!
But the great Colonel Sneelock is just the right kind
Of a man who can tame him. I'm sure he won't mind.

Then I'll let Sneelock off for a few minutes' rest
While high over your heads you will see the best best
Of the world's finest, fanciest Breezy Trapeezing!
My Zoom-a-Zoop Troupe from West Upper Ben-Deezing
Who never quite know, while they zoop and they zoom,
Whether which will catch what one, or who will catch whom
Or if who will catch which by the what and just where,
Or just when and just how in which part of the air!

Ei! Ei! What a circus! My Circus McGurkus!
My workers *love* work. They say, "Work us! Please work us!
We'll work and we'll work up so many surprises
You'd never see half if you had forty eyses!"

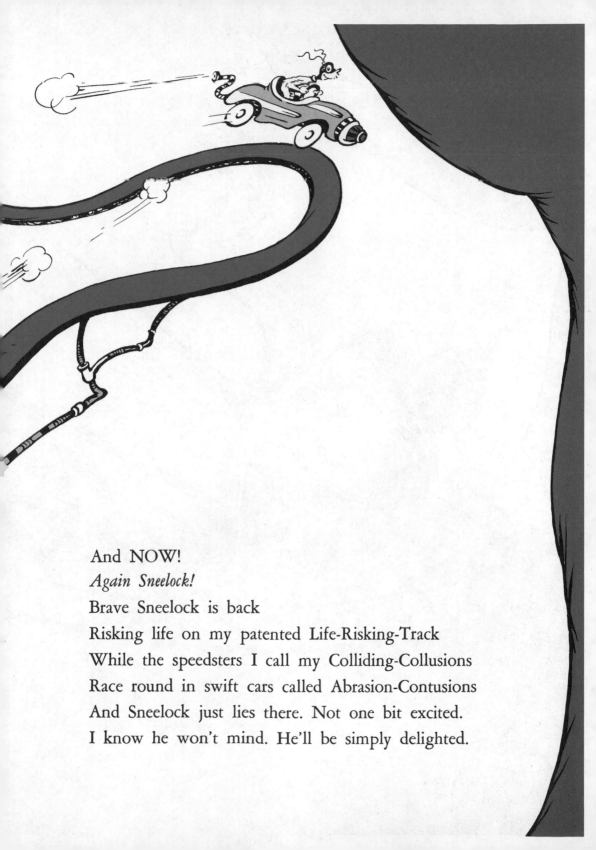

And NOW!
Again Sneelock!
Brave Sneelock is back
Risking life on my patented Life-Risking-Track
While the speedsters I call my Colliding-Collusions
Race round in swift cars called Abrasion-Contusions
And Sneelock just lies there. Not one bit excited.
I know he won't mind. He'll be simply delighted.

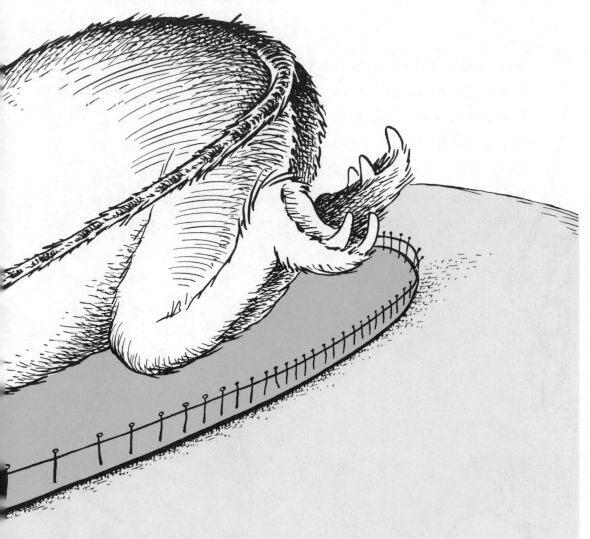

And *here,* in a contest of brute-strength and muscle,
Kid Sneelock, my champ-of-all-champs, will now tussle
And wrestle a beast called the Grizzly-Ghastly
And slap him around! Then he'll slam him down fastly
And pin both his shoulders tight flat to the mat.
Kid Sneelock will love it! I'm sure about that.

And while THAT goes on THERE, look at THIS go on HERE!
Have you heard of my herd of "Through-Horns-Jumping-Deer"...?
Every deer jumps through horns of another pell-mell
While *his* horns are jumped through at the same time as well
By a deer whose horns ALSO are being jumped through
By another who's having HIS horns jumped through, too,
Which I'm *sure* Trainer Sneelock can train them to do.

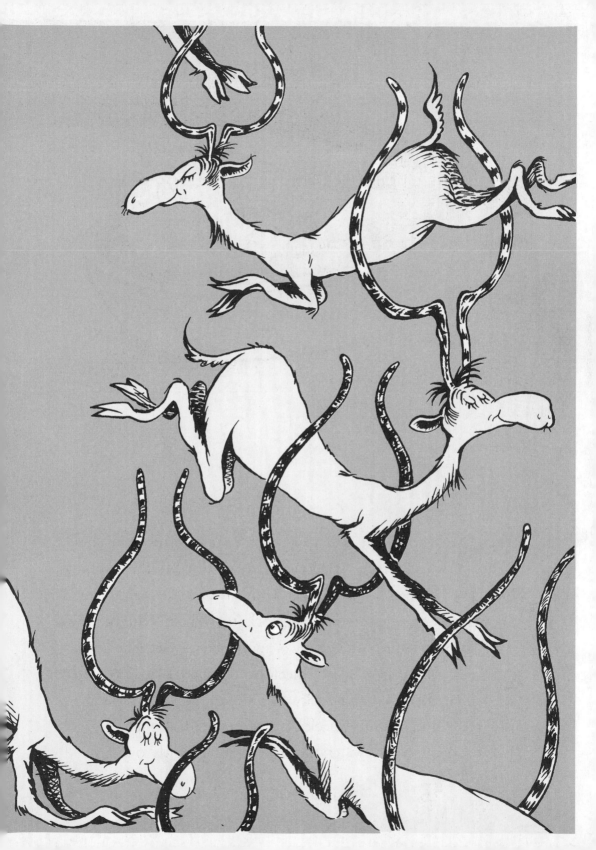

Then the whole tent will ring with hoorays and wild shouts
When I wheel in my whales and they turn on their spouts!
First my Whale Number One, with an aim that aims true
Spouts a spout that spouts Sneelock to Whale Number Two!
And then Whale Number Two spouts his spout like a gun
And *that* spout spouts old Sneelock right back to Whale One!
And then forwards and backwards on spout after spout
My great Spout-Rider Sneelock gets spouted about
Just as long as the water they're spouting holds out!

Then my Tournament Knights! Noble apes without fears!
Sir Hector! Sir Vector! Sir Bopps! And Sir Beers!
Sir Hawkins! Sir Dawkins! Sir Jawks! And Sir Jeers!
Clatter into the tent, and while everyone cheers
Stage a roust-about-joust with their boxing glove spears!

And while all this wild ruckus-ing goes on below,
At the top of the tent . . . look! The star of my show!
Great Daredevil Sneelock! The world's bravest type!
He comes pulled through the air by three Soobrian Snipe
On a dingus contraption attached to his pipe!
And while people below are all turning chalk white
And all biting their fingernails off in their fright,
Great Sneelock soars up to a terrible height!

Then he shakes himself loose!
He starts down in a dive
Such as no man on earth
Could come out of alive!
But he smiles as he falls
And no fear does he feel.
His nerves are like iron,
His muscles like steel.
And he plunges! Down! Down!
With his hair still combed neat
Four thousand, six hundred
And ninety-two feet!

Then he'll land in a fish bowl.
He'll manage just fine.
Don't ask *how* he'll manage.
That's *his* job. Not mine.

Why! He'll be a Hero!
Of *course* he won't mind
When he finds that he has
A big circus behind.